In Remembrance of the Master:
KIRPAL SINGH

He it is that speaks within me
He it is to whom I speak
He does all
He is all
If we might see Him

THE SONG OF EVERYTHING

THE SONG OF

EVERYTHING *and other stories*

By TRACY LEDDY

illustrated by
Rixford Jennings

THE SANT BANI PRESS Tilton, N. H. *1975*

THE STORIES

THE SONG OF EVERYTHING

THE SONG OF EVERYTHING

O NCE THERE WAS a poor man who made his living carrying supplies between his own village at the foot of a mountain and another village near its summit. On one day he might carry a load of corn or wheat, on another a basket of bricks, on another packets of nails or tea. His load could be almost anything. It did not matter to the man for he had a strong back and a good wife who looked after him.

One morning the man awoke and prepared himself for his usual journey. He stood up from his bed to go in by the fire for his morning tea and instead, fell flat on his back with a groan. Never in his life had he felt so weak. It seemed as though he was weighted down with many huge bundles, any one of them heavier than anything he had ever carried before.

He called to his wife, "Come, help me. Take some of this load off my back. I cannot get up. I can hardly move." His wife came running from the fire and stood drying her hands on her scarf. "What are you talking about, husband?" she asked, "I can see nothing on your back. You must get up and go out to the village. We need firewood and oil for dinner." The man struggled mightily to raise himself from the bed but he could not. Again he begged his wife to help him. She gave him both her hands and pulled and pulled but when he still could not be moved, she shrugged her shoulders and went back to her work, puzzled by her good husband's strange behavior. Then his two strong sons came and pulled and pulled and they could do nothing.

News of his strange malady traveled fast through the little village and pretty soon some of the man's friends appeared at the door to stare at him. They sniggered among themselves, looking at him lying down helpless and completely mystified. "Look at him!" they jeered, "such a sturdy fellow to have become suddenly so weak. Must be tired of working, ha!" and they went away.

At his wife's insistence, the village doctor came to examine him. He felt the man all over, looked into his eyes, his ears and his mouth, coughed a little and told the man and his wife that there was nothing wrong.

Weeks passed and the man's condition remained the same. Each day he struggled to rise from his bed only to fall back, exhausted and gasping under the weight he felt on his shoulders. More and more people in the village began to ridicule him. His wife began to neglect him and in the end would give him barely enough to eat. In despair the man told his sons to carry his bed out into a neighboring field where he could at least die in peace.

Some days later he was still groaning under the load which no one could see when across the field came a small child, singing. The man listened and listened. He had never heard such music. It made the sky bluer and the grass greener and the heat of the sun an embrace. It made him happy. It made him forget his heavy load. As the child came slowly towards him, the man, with great difficulty, lifted his head to look at him. Never had he seen a more beautiful face. Never had he seen more joyfilled eyes. And the song poured out of the child like his breath, never stopping, always changing until it seemed to the man that the child was the song.

"What is that music you are singing, little brother?" asked the man feebly. "I have heard nothing so beautiful ever before."

"My song is the song of everything," replied the child, and then added sweetly, "shall I teach it to you?"

"Oh, yes," begged the man, "for if I could sing it, even just a little of it, I feel I could die in peace despite my heavy load."

The child smiled down at the man on the bed. "My song will not help you to die, brother," he said gently, "It will surely help you to live." And he began at once to teach the man his song.

For many days the man remained on his bed in the field learning the child's song. And as he took the music deeper and deeper into his heart, it seemed the air around them was filled with the sweetest of sounds, with harps and horns, with flutes and trumpets and drums. At last the man himself began hesitantly to sing. With each passing day as he sang and sang he felt less and less of the burden on his shoulders until finally, almost without realizing it, he could stand again and stretch and walk around.

One bright morning the child smiled at the man and said, "I must be leaving you for I think you know my song well enough now and there are others who must learn it. Sing it deep in your heart until the end of your days and you will always be happy." And with a last joyous glance at the man, the child went singing on his way.

Tears stood in the man's eyes as he watched until the child was lost from view among the trees at the edge of the field. Then, with a sigh, he turned and carried his bed back into his house and went out to work as usual. His family and friends who had all but forgotten about him were astonished by the sight of him. Full of a secret joy he went about his work carrying bricks and corn and nails or sat among the villagers or took his meals or played with all the children. The man kept the child's song deep in his heart for the rest of his life and the power of it made him loved by all who saw him.

As he lay dying, a very old man, people came from miles around to stand sorrowfully at his bedside. His wife and sons wept, but his luminous eyes never changed as he smiled up at them. With his last breath he opened his mouth and began to sing. The little room was soon filled with the sweetest of sounds, with bells and vina, with flutes and drums and the people around him were filled with a strange peace.

"My brothers, my sisters, hear me," said the old man, "this is the song of everything. Do not weep for I'm going to become part of that song."

WE ARE ALL ONE

W HEN SHE WAS young, the girl Kamla wanted to be like every living thing around her. She wanted to have feathers and wings. She wanted to have four legs and fur. She wanted to have blossoms and leaves. If she saw an apple hanging from a branch she thought, "What would it be like to be big and round and ripening in the hot sun, I wonder." And if she saw chipmunks at their games, she thought, "What would it be like to have three black stripes down my back and a fluffy tail and to scurry around all the time, I wonder."

Her mother used to tell her not to bother her head about such things. After all, she could do nothing about it; why not enjoy her own human form? But her father used to say to her quite seriously, "We are all one, I tell you,

Kamla; we are all one. Someday you will know this thing in your own heart."

Kamla spent much of her time in her father's gardens, learning the names of the trees and flowers from the old gardener and watching the many little creatures who lived there. Toads, lizards, parrots, monkeys, beetles, butterflies, dahlias, marigolds, she treated each as a special friend and loved them all.

Often she sat near the brook at the bottom of the garden and stared up at the tall green mountains which nearly surrounded her father's house. "What would it be like to feel the clouds come down to cover me and shut out the sky, I wonder," she would say to herself and gaze thoughtfully at the surging mists. Then Kamla would sigh and remind herself, "We are all one. My father says that to me all the time and I know he's right but I still don't know it in my own heart. Not yet." And she went right on wondering what it would be like to be everything around her.

One afternoon Kamla stood at the big red and white gate at the front of the house and watched some monkeys chase each other up and down the huge old banyan tree on the opposite side of the road. "What would it be like," she began again and then stopped. She shook her head, turned, and walked slowly back to the house. For once she was tired of wondering. No one was around. Her mother had gone out to the bazaar and her father's doors were closed. The old gardener had gone up to the village to visit his sick grandson. Bored and a little sad, Kamla lay down on a rope bed on the veranda and fell into a deep sleep.

The clouds rolled in and soon a terrific thunderstorm shook the house in the valley. Curtains of rain streamed off the rooftops. Water gurgled in the gutters and spattered into pools in the gravel, but Kamla slept on.

Oddly enough, it was only when the rainbow appeared that she awoke quite reluctantly, as though from a very beautiful dream she did not want to forget, a dream so vivid that it still lingered in her eyes as she looked about her. To Kamla, the whole world seemed more real than ever before and the sight of the double rainbow in the field across the road seemed to deepen her impression. She wandered through her father's dripping gardens, looking around her as though for the very first time.

Suddenly she stopped, looked down at her feet and stared in dismay. Just beside her bare toes, an army of ants had surrounded a large earthworm which had been stranded among the stones by the storm. They were closing in to devour him. Instantly Kamla felt fire flicker all over her body, as though a thousand tiny mouths were biting into her own soft flesh. Without stopping to think, she ran to the well, pumped a bucket full of water, dashed back and poured it all over the worm and its attackers. Immediately she felt cool and refreshed, as though her body had never known what it was like to be wet before.

Completely routed, the waterlogged ants staggered unsteadily in all directions. The worm slithered into a near-by puddle. And Kamla sat down in the middle of the gravel path and laughed and cried.

THE SNAKE CHARMER

INDEED, everyone agreed he was a most unusual snake charmer. He carried no baskets of trained cobras with him as he traveled up and down the world and would accept no money for his performances, yet he seemed able to charm away more snakes than anyone else. No one knew where he came from or where he had been; no one could predict when he would arrive or dissappear. He came when he was called, he told someone once, merrily, that's all.

And he was a strange looking fellow, too; thin and tall and very dark. He wore a ragged woolen cloak that had once been white and a tattered turban that had suffered a similar fate. His shoes were long and pointed; one sole was partly separated from the rest of the shoe and it made a curious flapping sound, almost like a bird's wings, whenever he took a step. When he wasn't playing his vina he was smiling like a small child. People everywhere loved to see him coming; once they saw him they completely forgot all about his odd appearance and only listened to his music which was unlike any other music in the world.

Few people ever really noticed his deep-set eyes under the black curls and tattered turban but those who did never forgot them. I shall tell you about three who saw.

It happened that the snake charmer arrived one summer's day in a small mountain village that nestled into a steep hillside just under another higher range of mountains. It was a surprisingly fertile place and very peaceful; the people there lived in considerable harmony and were generally kind to strangers.

As word of his coming passed quickly from house to house, the villagers began to gather to hear the snake charmer play. The women left their sweeping and washing; the men left their scythes and carts, their dreams and papers and came out of the fields and shops to listen. As he made his way slowly up the steep and narrow cobbled street, the music he played sounded so sweetly upon his listeners' ears that old men in tea shops found themselves weeping and little children stood motionless at their games.

Two old women sat knitting in the sunlight by the side of the road. One had been complaining very bitterly for the hundredth time about her nearest neighbor but the sound of the approaching procession interrupted her gossip. When she looked up, the snake charmer was standing before her and staring straight into her eyes. His music grew sweeter and sweeter still; there were voices in it now and they seemed to be calling to the woman from somewhere very far away. With a joy and terror she had never known, the old woman stuffed her knitting into the bib of her long black apron and scrambled to her feet. As soon as she stood up, snakes began to appear from under her hair and from beneath her tongue, little ones, swiftly moving, black and livid green.

For just moments they were visible to the horrified villagers and the old woman and then they were wriggling into the snake charmers's pockets and gone. The snake charmer took his vina out of his mouth and smiled at the old woman. Unable to resist, she in turn looked steadily back into his eyes. But she saw no ordinary eyes with iris and pupil; she saw only light, the most brilliant light she had ever seen, far brighter than the sun and much warmer. As she continued staring, she felt that warmth envelop her, fill her down to the inside of her wrinkled old toes. Silently she bowed her head.

Suddenly she was moved to look up; she caught sight of her neighbor's face in the hushed and wondering crowd. She burst into tears and pushed her way through the villagers until she could embrace the other woman. "I'm a wretched old crone," she sobbed, "forgive me, sister, I'll never speak ill of you again." The other woman was too surprised to answer but she felt some of her neighbor's

inexplicable warmth and sat down with her and comforted her.

The snake charmer put his vina to his lips and walked
on.

Further along the road stood an abandoned temple and
beside it, a house with a very beautifully decorated facade.
The doors were of sandalwood, richly carved, and the walls
were painted with lions and peacocks. It belonged to the
wealthiest man in the village, a widower whose only
daughter had looked after his household for many years.
As the snake charmer stepped lightly along the cobble-
stones, one shoe flapping like a bird's wing, the daughter's
shrill voice could be heard above the music, scolding the
servants at their tasks as usual. She was a proud girl who
would have been beautiful had she not been so lonely and
dissatisfied with her life.

In a moment of domestic silence, the snake charmer's
music struck her ears for the first time. It was merry and
joyful and spoke of great happiness to come. Feeling curiously drawn to it, the girl stood out on the balcony in all
her fine clothes to watch the snake charmer pass by. But
when he came abreast of the house, instead of continuing
on his way he stopped and, playing with all his heart, he
stared straight up at her. The girl hung over the balcony
to hear the music more clearly and suddenly she was astonished to hear a hissing sound all around her. All her
jewelry, earrings, necklace, bracelets and bangles had
turned into tiny snakes, white ones and brilliant red and

gold ones. She and the villagers watched, thunderstruck, as they all slithered over the pierced balustrade and into the snake charmer's pockets where they were seen no more.

The snake charmer took his vina out of his mouth and smiled up at the rich man's daughter. Strangely relieved and happy for the first time in her life, she looked back steadily into the snake charmer's eyes. She saw no ordinary eyes with iris and pupil; she saw only stars in a clear night sky, stars more brilliant than any she had ever seen from her father's roof. And, like the old woman, she too was suddenly filled with warmth from her shining black hair to her sandaled feet. "I must go and help them in the kitchen," she said to herself, "perhaps I've been too harsh with them. Perhaps they don't understand what it is I want them to do." And she danced down the stairs and out into the garden to pick flowers for her father's table at lunch.

The snake charmer put his vina to his lips and walked on. A smiling, silent crowd followed him. As he passed one poor dwelling near the edge of the village, a tapping, shuffling sound could be heard coming from a flight of stone stairs inside. The snake charmer stopped once more and stood quietly by the door, playing and playing, his long fingers quick as butterflies on his hollow vina. The tune was sad now, at once haunting and pleading and full of promises of great joy.

After a few minutes a pale young boy stumbled out of the doorway. One of his legs was withered and he leaned upon a crudely-made crutch. A murmur of approval burbled through the crowd for the boy was well-known in the village. He had a good heart and spent most of his time playing with the little children. He never complained about his withered leg or about his absent mother; he had done his best to look after his old father until he died, just a few weeks before. And more than one of the villagers had remarked on the still, distant look that often crossed his face. He limped straight toward the snake charmer and fell at his feet. "I've been waiting for so long," he said, weeping, "I thought you would never come."

The snake charmer stopped playing. He stooped down and lifted the boy gently to his feet with one strong brown arm. "Catch hold of my cloak," he cried merrily, "and off we'll go!" And again the snake charmer began to play.

A man stood on his roof waving a stick at some monkeys in a banyan tree next to his house. "They are stealing my guavas," he grumbled to the bystanders and then, as the strains of the snake charmer's music floated back to him, he grinned a little foolishly and put down his stick. "I guess there are enough for all of us, my brothers," he said and went back inside.

Some of the children laughed to see the monkeys leap with a clatter from tin rooftop to rooftop, the ripe green fruits bulging from their mouths. But not the crippled boy. He had eyes only for the snake charmer and ears only for his music. He held on tightly to the snake charmer's cloak and followed him right out of the village.

The crowd watched the boy limp off with the snake

charmer and many are sure they saw the crutch disappear, black and wriggling, into the snake charmer's pocket and the boy's stride become steadier and steadier as they walked along into the mists.

High up in the mountains the snake charmer stopped to rest. He turned to look the boy full in the face. The boy stared back straight into his eyes. At first he could see only the bluest of skies, but as he looked deeper inside them, he could see the snake charmer himself sitting in a ring of fire, playing his vina.

"Do you want to see more?" asked the snake charmer with a smile. "Oh yes!" answered the boy without hesitation. And the snake charmer began again to play. As he played, it seemed to the boy that the snake charmer began to grow. He grew and grew until at last he blotted out the entire landscape, the mountains, the valley and the sky and always he played, bending closer and closer to the enraptured boy. Then the music became a wind, a whirling cone of sound which pulled and pulled at the boy until finally he found himself deep, deep inside the snake charmer's vina and walking joyfully toward the snake charmer in the ring of fire who would play for him forever.

Then the snake charmer put his vina to his lips and walked on.

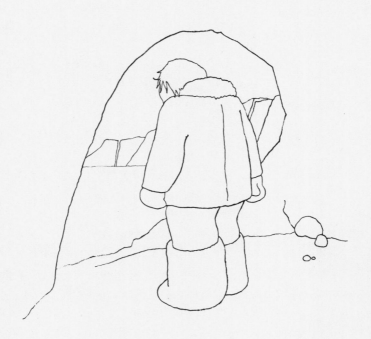

THE STORY OF THE ICE GIANT

*The princess wants and does not want to be
rescued.—Jung.*

ONCE, IN THE FROZEN wastelands at the very top of the
world, a momentous discovery was made. A young ice
giant, out alone in an icefield just after dawn, noticed that
in sunlight, even the weak, pale, hazy light that shone only
some of the time in that far-off land, his body cast no
shadow. At the same time, he noticed that the air around
him was filled with sound, a high, subtle kind of music
which vibrated through him from head to foot and caused
him to nearly faint with ecstasy. It was a terrifying experience. For those few moments he felt as though he
didn't exist, or, if he did, it was only as a listening ear,
straining with all its strength to catch more and more of
the music.

Beside himself with fear, the ice giant shut his eyes and covered his ears with his fur-mittened hands. He threw himself down against a wall of ice and lay there cowering and shaking and moaning to shut out the sound. He began to pinch himself and kick himself. He bit his lips and strained his muscles to reassure himself that he was still alive.

When the sun went behind a low-lying bank of clouds, the ice giant jumped to his feet and lumbered back across the icefield. Whimpering like a lost cub, he stumbled into the cavern among the other ice giants of his tribe and jibbered, "What evil has befallen me that my body casts no shadow in the light? Is it true of all of us? Have we all lost our shadows?" The others roared with laughter and ill-concealed derision. "Whatever is the young one talking about?" they shouted to each other, "Everyone, everything has a shadow." "But have you noticed yours lately, brother, or yours, cousin?" persisted the young giant, still trembling. "Don't be so foolish," they retorted, "We're far too busy with other things to stop and attend to such trivial matters as whether or not we cast shadows." And with many oaths and grumblings, for they had quickly ceased to be amused by the young giant's obvious fear, the tribe of ice giants returned to their work dismembering several dozen polar bears for breakfast.

Watching them, the young ice giant felt a definite queasiness growing in his stomach and he turned away without eating. Somehow he managed to pass a quiet day, out of the sun and undisturbed by the chaffings or disgruntled looks of his kinsmen, his mind filled with his experience in the icefield and with the strange, terrible and ecstatic feeling of not being. An icy chill seized his whole body whenever he remembered it, but curiously enough, he found that that brief moment was all he wanted to think about during the entire day.

When darkness fell, he curled up in a ball, a ten-foot, large-framed, bearskin-clothed person who looked for all the world like an enormous white hedgehog asleep in his cavern of ice.

That night the ice giant had a wonderful dream. It had two parts to it; one was very peaceful but the other was quite disturbing. The first part of his dream was of a vast, silent landscape, a huge expanse, a yellow desert plain that stretched as far as the eye could see under a brilliant golden sky. Light was everywhere. The atmosphere above the golden sand was filled with tiny, winking particles, vivid and separate as snowflakes or grains of sand but much less dense than either. There was a familiar sound in the air, a high, subtle kind of music that seemed to come from the light. It was utterly calm there, totally serene. It filled the giant's heart with a great peace; for a fleeting moment he wanted to remain there, always.

Then, in the giant's dream, he suddenly heard his own voice speaking. It rumbled forth plaintively saying, "How empty this place is! Where am *I*?" and as soon as those words were spoken, the scene began to change. A tiny black speck appeared in the middle of the golden plain. As the giant watched, the speck grew larger and larger; it seemed to be propelled by tremendous force toward the near edge of the plain. On and on it came, casting an enormous shadow before it. Eventually the landscape itself began to change. Close to the giant's angle of vision at the near edge of the desert, large sand dunes appeared, and then rocks, too, strangely shaped and deeply incised by wind and sand. Nearer and nearer the moving object came and the ice giant suddenly realized with a shock that it was speedily growing into himself, a huge, bearskin-clothed ice giant, heavy as stone. His own image came very close and found itself at the outer-most edge of the desert. It became increasingly entangled in the dense thicket which grew there, covered with cobwebs and seemingly impenetrable as stone. With great effort, the giant's image struggled through to the near side of the thicket and fell down in darkness into a deep, deep sleep.

The ice giant awoke with a feeling of great sadness and loss in his heart. He was overwhelmed with inexpressible longings and he knew no peace. He crawled slowly out of his cavern and looked around him. There was a faint tinge of light low in the sky; everything was cold and still. Only the north wind was abroad, shifting ghosts of snow from one icy slope to another. The giant stood quietly. The sense of loss and longing in his heart did not seem to be lessening. The north wind became a little stronger, strong enough to blast the ice giant his first few hesitant steps in a general, southerly direction, "This is no place for me," the ice giant said to himself at last, "I must find somewhere else to live, a place where I can forget about ice-fields and dreams and never stand in the sun again." And off he trudged, before dawn, without saying so much as goodbye to any of his snoring relations.

Thus began the ice giant's long journey. Little by little, he progressed out of the frozen wasteland at the top of the world that had been his home and into the mountains, forests and cities of the warmer regions of the earth. He traveled far and wide, his footsteps leading him in an arc from east to west, always moving in a southerly direction like a steadily plunging pendulum. He made his way slowly from place to place, seeking shelter from the sun by day wherever he could and venturing forth only by night or in the mist and rain.

He soon began to encounter people of all kinds who stared at his huge, shaggy shape, observed his still, sad face and reacted in a variety of ways. Some people hated him on sight, some ridiculed him and some feared him greatly. A few took pity on the hulking wanderer with eyes fixed unwaveringly on some distant point and made him welcome. For the most part, the ice giant ignored those who hated him or made fun of him and tried to stay away from those who feared him so as not to trouble their hearts unnecessarily. And for the hospitality of the people who treated him with kindness, he was deeply grateful.

In any place he stopped, the ice giant proved himself a

willing and resourceful worker. Once he helped the people of a tiny hamlet in a remote valley to repair their church steeple which had been struck by lightning in a recent storm. And once he stood all night in the dark recesses of a mine-tunneled mountain holding up some faulty beams until all the miners who had been trapped there could scramble out to safety. He helped to build bridges, rescue animals, harvest crops. He would take nothing but a little food in return for any work he did, although more than once it took two or three whole wheels of some farm wife's good cheese to make him aware that he had put anything into his stomach at all. People gradually became accustomed to seeing the ice giant at work in the night and the rain and ceased to comment on it or to think it strange behavior. But the prospect of a life in perpetual darkness began to sadden the giant greatly; the sense of loss he had felt so acutely after his dream began to plague his working hours, began to become a permanent part of his life as he walked about the world. Still, his fear was greater than his longing and he steadfastly stayed out of the sun.

Three times the ice giant thought he had stopped for good, having found at last the peaceful place he sought so diligently. Once he stopped among some friendly shepherds in a mountain pass, once among some forest dwellers and once among the amiable folk of a large and bustling market town. But in vain did the ice giant look for peace and forgetfulness in nature or in friendship and festivals, for each time he began to feel himself sinking happily into the natural rhythm of his surroundings, he again had the dream he was trying so hard to forget. And each time he awoke from it, he was filled with a renewed and intensified sense of loss and knew he must move on.

After waking from the dream for the third time, the realization came to him that fearful, yes, terrified as he was of the sun and of the experience in which he was forced to see that his body cast no shadow, he knew at last in the depths of his heart that it was indeed nothing other than the sun he was longing for, that nothing else mattered in his life and that he would have no lasting peace until he stood, fully conscious, in the landscape of his wonderful, terrible dream.

Increasingly wearily, the ice giant wandered on, always in a southerly direction, propelled now by the north wind, now by the unseen sun. One night, tired of walking and sick at heart, the ice giant stumbled against a thick wall and could go no further. "I may as well rest here," he murmured to himself, then added, "for that matter, I may as well die." And he lay down and closed his eyes.

That night, the ice giant had another dream. He dreamed he lay in the shadow of a great tangled thicket, covered with cobwebs and seemingly impenetrable as stone. He dreamed he wept bitter tears and wished with all his heart for the courage to go out, just once, and stand in the sunlight. And in his dream he was suddenly propelled with tremendous ease up, up and over the great tangled thicket and then over strangely shaped rocks and sand-dunes until before his eyes stretched a vast, silent landscape, a huge expanse, a yellow desert plain under a brilliant golden sky.

Warmth woke him slowly. He stirred in his sleep, rolled over and sat up, rubbing his eyes. There was no wall in front of him; there was nothing facing him but an empty plain filled with light. Before him lay a great dark shadow and it took him some moments to realize it was his own. And a sound was in the air, a sound he recognized with great joy. It was a high, subtle music that made him strain with all his strength to listen.

With the music pouring through him and all around him and the bright air filled with filaments of light, the ice giant suddenly knew exactly what it was he had to do. With his heart beating like thunder, he began resolutely to walk toward the middle of the plain. Under that relentless sun, it was as though he were really melting. He had a sense of diminishing, of the sand rushing up to him as he moved faster and faster toward one certain spot in the plain, of light swirling around him like a storm of tiny candles until he could no longer tell where the sand left off and the sky began.

Then all at once he stopped and looked down. His shadow was completely gone. At last he could not feel the blistering heat on his back and head, or the fiery sand beneath his feet. At last he could not feel.

At last he was part of the light.

MICHAEL IN THE HOUSE
OF THE SUN

Lips pursed in a whistle, hands stuffed into overall pockets, bare feet kicking up the dust along the side of the road, Michael was on his way home after a long day on his uncle's farm. There had been corn and beets and a salad from the garden for lunch and fresh raspberries and cream besides; the life that was in those good things had joined with the life that was in the boy to fill him with strength and song. It was late, but not too late that hot August afternoon and Michael strode along, looking all around him and enjoying everything he saw. Suddenly he was moved to stop in the middle of the empty road and throw his arms wide.

"Hullo, Father Sun!" he shouted up into the sky. "How glad I am you make things grow like corn and frogs and

boys like me!" and then, in another outburst, he cried,
"How I wish I could come to live with you always!"

And in that summer stillness, it seemed as though the
sun came down out of the sky, burning and burning, until
it hovered in the air just above Michael's head. A human
form with a radiant face stepped out of the sun and stood
before Michael who gaped at him with pounding heart,
feeling as though he had come too close to a roaring fire.
Wordlessly he waited to see what would happen next.

The splendid figure spoke, "You will be quite welcome
in the Father's house, Michael, but not just yet. There is
another place you must go to first and how long you will
live there only God knows. Are you willing?"

"Yes," Michael whispered to the face of fire, "Oh, yes!"

"Good," said the figure to the boy, "One thing more,
remember me. All the time you are in the other place,
think of me. Things will go better for you if you do. And
Michael," continued he, "In case you were wondering, I
and the Father are the same."

With a long, searching look at Michael, the figure
stepped back into the light and disappeared. And then the
sun climbed back into the sky and set behind the western
hills as it did on any other day.

Like one struck blind, Michael could not bring himself
to move for a while. Then he began to run down the road.
"Hooray! Hooray!" he shouted into the evening birdsong,
"I'm going to live in the house of the sun!" and then he
stopped running and was quiet, remembering the other

place the sun had spoken of and wondering what would happen next.

When he arrived home, Michael found a cold supper of bread and cheese and peaches laid out on the kitchen table with a note from his mother. The note said that the rest of the family had gone to the city for the day and would be back late.

Relieved at finding himself alone, Michael sat down and ate without thinking of his food, his mind on his conversation with the sun. A great feeling of warmth and joy spread through his body and it seemed to remind him, to remind every particle of him, remember me!

When Michael awoke slowly from sleep the next morning, he could hear someone snoring but the sound seemed to come from very far away. He was in pitch darkness and all he could hear was this strange breathing. Suddenly two small windows shot open, both facing in the same direction, out and a little down.

"That's odd," thought Michael, "There are my feet sticking out at the bottom of the bed-clothes and there's the birch tree outside my bedroom window and there's my hand coming up to rub my . . . why, I'm the one who's been snoring and those windows are my eyes!"

Think of it. It was a little like suddenly discovering that you lived on the top floor of a three-storey building, only the first floor could move around and the second floor could think and the third floor, where you really lived, was in total darkness; you could not even imagine how far apart the walls were, the darkness was so deep.

For Michael, however, this darkness did not last for very long. Recovering from the shock of his new situation, Michael's body got up and dressed itself and started down the stairs for breakfast. On his way, Michael passed his little brother's room and his mind quickly remembered how much he wanted to punch him for not sharing the sweets their grandmother had sent them a day or so before. Instantly there was an ugly picture on one wall in the dark room, a moving picture of a small boy and a big boy fighting. The small boy was crying and the big boy had such a puffy, nasty grin on his face.

"Oh," cried Michael in the dark room, "Just look at that bully. He's really enjoying hurting the little boy. Why," he gasped in sudden, painful recognition, "that bully's me!"

This was, admittedly, a bad way to begin the day and Michael's answer to his mother's cheery "Good morning!" was a barely audible, "Hullo."

And it got worse. It seemed to Michael that everything he did or said or thought all day was thrown upon the giant screen in the dark room where he lived. He found himself, in just one day, looking at so many pictures so foolish and so ugly he could hardly recognize them, yet that was exactly what he had to do. And always, in each one, the villain was none other than himself.

As the days went on, the pictures grew in number and unpleasantness until the dark room was filled with images, and Michael began to feel helpless and bewildered and increasingly desperate for a way out. One day Michael thought, "I know what, I'll just sit down and close the windows." And he threw himself down in the tall grass behind his house and shut his eyes. But the pictures did not go away; they merely changed. Michael was forced to look at incidents of an hour ago, a month ago or a year ago, of his bad temper, his criticism of his friends, his laziness, his greed and on and on.

Michael became so disgusted by these pictures of himself, so very different from the way he was used to seeing himself, if indeed he had thought about himself at all, that he would gladly have died and put an end to it then and there, but he was suddenly moved to remember what the sun had told him. "Think of me," he had recommended, "Things will go better for you if you do." And Michael sat up in the grass and closed his eyes and thought of the sun and of the face like living fire.

Wonder of wonders, as soon as his thoughts in the dark room turned toward the sun, the pictures began to fade. And in the months that followed, Michael soon discovered that the more attention he put on the sun, the fewer and less ugly the pictures that confronted him.

At night sometimes, the sun assumed his human form and visited Michael in his dreams to encourage and console him while he lived in the dark room. The radiant figure would sit with Michael and tell him all the ways to avoid making the ugly pictures. He would laugh with him and give him little presents or tell him stories about his other children or stroke Michael's brow to chase away all his sadness. Before he left him, the figure would remind the sleeping boy, "Remember me!" Michael awoke from such dreams feeling stronger and more determined than ever to deal with the ever present images in the dark room and he would think of the sun with greater fervor than before.

Oh, he would have a very bad day every now and then when pictures seemed to stream into the dark room, but whenever this happened, and Michael was made to face yet another example of his meanness or of his boasting, he would cry aloud from his heart, "Oh, Father Sun, I do not want to be this way or talk this way or think this way any more. Please help me." And the sun's warmth would seize Michael and flow around him and through him until he began to think that the sun was inside him as well as outside.

As Michael began to change the way he acted and the way he spoke, according to the sun's directions, and kept his thoughts more and more on the sun, the number of pictures began to lessen quite noticeably. And as the pictures lessened, the darkness in the room also lessened. Little by little, light seemed to be seeping in through cracks and holes in the walls, small ones to begin with, but steadily widening. Michael spent most of his days now longing for the time when he could go to live in the house of the sun. Oh, he ate and he played like any other boy, but he was always thinking of the sun. And the dark room where he lived grew steadily brighter.

There came one day when Michael opened the two windows to look out and there were no pictures at all. When he closed the windows there were no pictures either. And his heart was at peace. Then, without his thinking about it, the dark room grew very bright. Warmer and brighter it became until it outshone the splendor of that August afternoon so long ago. Michael could hardly believe what was happening to him. Inside what used to be the dark room stood the sun and in the middle of that brilliant light, the face like living fire was smiling and bidding him welcome.

"You see, child of mine," He said gently, "You've really been in my house all along." He held out His hand to Michael. "Come," He said, "There's much more to see."

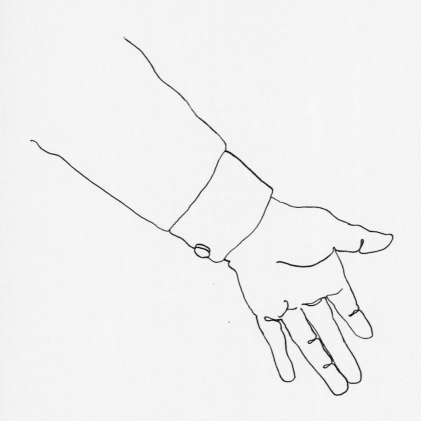

THE ROAD

WE WERE all sitting on the edge of the road, playing. I looked up and saw our father coming down the road toward us. I said to the others, "Oh, look, our father has come for us!" They also looked up, stared, and then laughed at me. "Don't be so silly," they said, "Nobody's there." And they went back to their games. But I saw him beckon and I heard him say, "Come, now. It's time for you to go home." And without another word to my friends, I stood up and took his outstretched hand and went away with him, walking slowly back up the road.

The others were very angry with me for leaving and threw dirt after me; they threatened me and jeered at me and called me names. I tried not to listen, not to care, and kept right on walking beside our father, my hand in his.

After a long while, my favorite companion ran up breathlessly and tried to catch hold of my other hand. I looked up at our father, "Is it all right?" "Yes," he said, "It's all right." I gladly took one of my companion's hands in my free hand and then he was able to see our father, too. So the three of us continued walking up the road.

Eventually, all our friends came up, one by one, until we were all holding hands and smiling and walking slowly together up the road with our father.

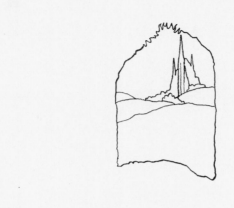

MAEVE

HAVING BEEN BORN a princess, Maeve had always had everything her heart desired. Up to the age of eighteen she had literally danced her way through life with a constant smile and a never-faltering step until one night something happened to her which changed her, completely.

It was after a great festival. Maeve had played songs of her own composition before her father, the king, and all his court. She had danced all night with many partners and had been celebrated as having the most beautiful face in the kingdom. The court had whispered of marriage for her soon.

Maeve had gone to bed, tired but elated with a sense of her growing fame. But this night the hours went by and she could not sleep. The noises in the palace around her gradually diminished until they ceased altogether. All was silent and still the princess could not sleep. She tossed and turned, trying to recapture the gaiety of the evening, her companions' faces, her music, anything, all to no avail.

Then she began to hear one sound, the sound of someone sobbing bitterly. The voice was muffled, as though it came from very far away. Maeve lay still, wondering. Where was it coming from, this heartbroken weeping, where? And then, with a start which caused her to sit bolt upright in bed, Maeve recognized the origin of the sound. It was coming from somewhere deep, deep inside her own body. Heart pounding, she sat and listened with all her might.

"Let me out!" cried the voice, "Let me out!"

"Who are you?" whispered Maeve in a fright.

"I'm your Self," cried the voice despairingly, "Oh, won't you please let me out!"

"Don't be silly," said Maeve to the voice, "I'm myself. All I have to do is look in the mirror and I can see myself quite clearly."

"Oh, no, you can't," said the little voice, "You're just an endless collection of false faces. Let me out and I'll show you who you really are."

"Don't talk such nonsense," said Maeve, "Go away and leave me alone. I'm very tired and I just want to go to sleep."

"You hear me now, dear princess," the voice persisted, "and sleep will not come to you again until you let me out. I will be HEARD!" And the voice grew very loud and let out a piercing wail.

Maeve covered her ears in horror and thought, "If this continues, I shall surely go mad. I must leave the palace until I get rid of this wretched creature and then I will return." She crept out of bed, dressed quickly in a long loose robe, drew a woolen cloak over that and stole barefoot through the quiet halls, down the great stairs, out into the deserted palace gardens and through a little gate into the forest beyond.

Fortunately, there was a moon, but even if there hadn't been Maeve could have found her way. She knew the forest as well as the palace, having spent years exploring both. She knew trails and bowers, thickets and copses and this night was on her way to a favorite haunt, an old ruined tower at the far end of the forest. It was a neglected place; she had come upon it one day looking for shelter in a sudden storm. No one would think to look for her in such a forgotten corner.

At last Maeve was able to distinguish the large moss-covered rocks marking the entrance of the tower. She stepped toward them and sat down in the dark entrance facing the forest. "Now then," she said to her self, "What is it you want me to do?"

The voice cried out, louder than ever, "Let me out!"

"How can I do that?" Maeve asked.

"You must find a way, you must, you must!" cried the voice, and suddenly, as though a floodgate had been opened, it began in a torrent of words to tell the princess how long it had been a prisoner and how dreadfully it had suffered.

"Stop, stop!" Maeve cried after a time, "I've never heard such a sad story and I cannot bear to hear another word of it. Is there no one to help me to help you?" And she threw herself on the ground and sobbed and sobbed.

An unusual stillness pervaded the forest as a strange image suddenly passed before the princess' inner eye. She had become a castle and her face was the topmost tower. A long stair wound down and down through the tower to the most secret dungeon in the castle. A tiny figure of light lay inside that dungeon, a figure in chains, crumpled and sad. The figure was sobbing in despair when from outside the tower a long arm reached in and turned the key in the dungeon door. The figure rose and struggled to the door. It pushed the door open and stood, heavily laden, at the foot of the stair. Then it began to cry, "Let me out! Let me out!" The long arm from outside began to tear down the bricks one by one from the front of the tower and as each brick fell, a link in the shining figure's chain fell also, turned into a butterfly and flew away. The bricks fell, the figure climbed, until it reached the top of the stair where it stood, freed from all its chains, in the emptiness of the fallen bricks. At that precise moment, the entire castle melted into nothingness and all that remained in the vision of the princess was the figure of light.

At dawn a rustling in the intense stillness broke in upon

Maeve's tears and she looked up. Seated directly across from her in the shadows of an oak was an old man dressed in white whose face shone like the sun. His eyes were warm and wise as he looked at the princess. "Well met, Maeve," he said, "Your Self is indeed at the foot of the stair. That was no dream. Now, shall we begin?"

"Who are you?" whispered Maeve, awed at such a visitor in the most remote part of her father's forest.

The old man chuckled. "I am my Self," he replied.

"That voice which calls itself my self says I am only false faces," said Maeve. "He says that he is real and I am not. How can I find out if this is true?"

"Wait and see," said the old man. "Here, I'll show you." He scooped up a handful of earth from the ground in front of the princess. Immediately a shallow pool of clear water filled in the space. Not a ripple broke its surface. "Now look at your face, Maeve," he directed, "and tell me what you see."

Maeve leaned forward and looked into the pool at her reflection. What she saw was not the shining figure of her vision, nothing like it. Nor was it like the image she was used to admiring in any number of mirrors in the palace. What she saw in the pool was an expression, one of many hundreds that flitted across her features every day. "Oh!" she said, "I look so greedy. I look as though all I wanted was more chocolates when I'd already eaten half a box."

"Do you like to look like that?" asked the old man.

"No," murmured Maeve with tears in her eyes.

"Well then, take that expression off," said the old man.
Maeve put her hands up to her face and pulled and
pulled. Nothing happened. "You are making fun of me,"
she said to the old man.

"Not at all," he replied, "You might ask me to help."

Maeve bowed her head. "Please help me," she said.
"Obviously I cannot do this alone."

The old man reached forward across the pool and barely
touched the princess' face. A mask as thin as onionskin
fell into his palm, curled up and withered like a dead leaf
which he blew away. "Now Maeve," he said quietly, "Look
again into the pool. What do you see?"

Maeve leaned forward as she had before and studied
her reflection in the pool. "Oh," she said, "I look so lazy!
I look as though I had done nothing all day long and was
now unwilling to get up even to greet my father, the king."

"Do you like to look like that?" the old man asked.

"No," murmured Maeve with tears in her eyes.

"Well then, take that expression off too," said he.

"You do it, please," Maeve begged him, "I know now I
can do nothing without your help."

Again the old man reached forward across the pool. He
barely touched the princess' face. Another mask thin as
onionskin fell into his palm, curled up and withered like
a dead leaf which he blew away. "You must eat now before
we continue," said the old man, handing her a small basket of fruit and cheese and bread and nuts which he had
taken from behind the tree. Maeve took the food gratefully

and ate. Her companion sat, lost in his own thoughts, and waited for her to finish. Without a word Maeve handed the empty basket back to him and without a word he placed it behind the tree. Then, "Look again into the pool, Maeve," he directed, "and tell me what you see."

Days went by and each one followed the same pattern. When Maeve awoke in the morning, the old man was always there waiting for her. He would bring out the little basket filled with food and wait patiently while she ate. He would then direct her attention to her reflection in the pool. As soon as she recognized each expression, he lifted it from her face. The work was exhausting; she could see only a few expressions each day. When she tired, the old man would tell her to sleep; their work would begin again in the morning.

One night, in her mind's eye Maeve saw the image of the castle again. The tower was crumbling at a great rate and the figure of light was more than halfway up the stair. She awoke that morning happier than she had been in a long time.

But the expressions she saw in the pool became more and more subtle and therefore correspondingly difficult to identify. And soon there came a day when the old man watched with concern as she prepared to look into the pool. With good reason; she saw there an expression she had never seen before or imagined could exist in anyone. It was a ferocious look, a look of naked hatred and pride. It was her own face, stripped of all the outer masks, and it was dreadful to behold. The reflection held her and held her. A great shudder went through her body and she began to tremble violently. With all her strength she pulled her attention away from the hypnotic reflection and, after staring for a moment straight into the old man's eyes, she closed her own. Then three extraordinary things happened, all at the same time. The voice within her cried out louder than ever before, "Let me out!" and her own voice cried out "I do not want to die!" and the old man reached across the pool and touched her forehead and her head dropped like an overripe apple and splashed into the pool in front of her.

"Now I am nothing!" the princess shrieked, feeling only a great wind where her ears should have been.

"Not at all," said the old man, as he removed the princess' head from the pool. "Look again, Maeve, and see who you really are."

And Maeve leaned forward once more to look into the pool and saw only the figure of light staring back at her and his face shone like the sun. "But we're the same then, you and I," she gasped and stared at the old man.

"Of course we are," he chuckled, "For it is written, 'He it is that desireth in thee and He it is that is desired. He is all and He doth all if thou might see Him.' " And the two sat, no one knows for how long, oblivious and absorbed, smiling into each other's faces.

*   *   *

"What is that clamor I hear, my father?" asked Maeve,

"It is louder than all the noises of the forest."

"It is the cry of all the other prisoners in the world, begging to be released," answered the old man. "My daughter, you must go to them now and tell them what to do."

NATHAN

NATHAN had no idea what force or power had drawn him to this out-of-the-way spot, but here he was, walking slowly up a nameless dirt road in a far corner of the country, admiring deep woods radiant with October foliage on either side of him and feeling more wonderfully excited than he had ever felt in his life. At the turn in the road, he made his way rather shyly past the throngs of people near the old farmhouse and turned his steps toward the lane at one side of the house which ran down a small slope to an open space and a little pond. His inexplicable excitement mounted still higher when he saw the wooden house by the edge of the water; it looked so simple and comfortable, like a cottage built for a king. He joined some others who were sitting quietly on the grassy bank and his feeling of eager expectancy grew. He had spoken to no one, he had recognized no one, yet he felt completely at home in this peaceful place.

Eventually the door of the house opened and a man came out to greet the people waiting for him. Nathan studied him as he did most people he met and quickly decided he had never seen such a warm, compassionate face in all his many wanderings. The man was so natural and at the same time so dignified. Nathan became aware of how hushed his surroundings had become. No wind stirred the dry leaves in the cold, bright air; the clouds seemed to have stopped moving altogether. The very sky seemed to have come closer to the earth to listen to the man's soft words. He was saying,

"Once we all lived in the lap of God and now we are here on earth, imprisoned in the human form and unable to find our way back to our true home. What we need is someone who has freed himself from this earthly prison, someone who can also free us and guide us back to the lap of God Who is all bliss, all light and all joy."

With the man's first sentence, a wrenching pain entered Nathan's heart and remained there. He listened and listened, afraid to move, afraid to breathe for fear of missing one precious syllable of the words he had been so inexorably drawn to hear. And his heart grew sore within him. When the man's eyes, which roamed ceaselessly over all the faces upturned before him, alighted on Nathan, it seemed to him that a rainbow grew out of them and at-

tached itself to his own eyes, immediately establishing a
bond far stronger than the cord which had once bound him
to his mother. And in that moment, Nathan's heart was
lost forever to that power manifest in the man. "I am
yours; do with me what you will," he said in his heart to
the man. "Whatever you ask of me, no matter how difficult, I will obey. There is no other way for me to live,
now." The man gazed long into Nathan's eyes and then
continued speaking, "God says, I am the secret treasure
within you. Why don't you come and find me out?" Nathan said again in his heart, "Whatever you say, that shall
be my work."

As he sat staring up at the man, it seemed to Nathan
that the man sat in front of an open door, a huge door
which opened onto the only real world behind him. Some
old, old words were spoken deep inside him: "I am the
way, the truth and the light. No man cometh unto the
Father but by me." Nathan bowed his head to the ground,
his face wet with tears.

The next morning the man showed Nathan a glimpse of
that treasure of which he had spoken, so that Nathan
would be sure of what he was seeking. And it was as if a
great stone had been rolled away from the center of a
mountain and the splendor of many suns could be seen.
Nathan's breath was quite taken away. When the vision
had passed, Nathan's heart was wrung again inside him
and he vowed, "I will seek that light, all my life if I have
to, but I will dig it out." He took leave of the man after

thanking him for his gift and went back into the world to begin his work.

Nathan's life changed dramatically. Not that he had ever been strongly attached to the pleasures of this world, but now he would eat only the simplest food; he would read only the lives of other treasure-seekers. He didn't care what he did for work in the world to make his living; he kept to himself as much as possible, his attention on the wonderful light within him and on the man who had helped him to see it. When he had to be among people, he did his best to be friendly and helpful and loving, like the man who had helped him.

But it was a long, slow process. Most of the time there was no light, just a memory of it; there seemed to be a lithic density and heaviness to the darkness within him. He felt like a miner confronting an enormous mountain with only an ice pick and his bare hands . . . a mountain of desire, of seemingly endless self-deception, the mountain of himself. The digging was discouraging work. At times the mountain seemed impenetrable and he would cry out in anguish to the man for guidance. Each time he did so, some words would come singing into his heart to soothe him, "Be patient, Rome was not built in a day. You know there is light at the end of the tunnel. Don't despair. Take heart and dig deeper. Seek and ye shall find." And there would be a feeble ray, a glimmering of light through all the heavy rock and stone and he would remember the glorious light he had once seen and would continue with greater fervor than before. At one point, Nathan did discover that he had one other tool at his disposal, his attention. He found that the more keenly he bent his attention toward the work before him, the more deeply he penetrated into the mountain. It was like a laser beam in its effect.

For years Nathan dug and dug. His tunnel into the mountain of himself began to widen. He began to find the strength to lift obstructing boulders more and more easily. He also found that the more help he asked from the man the easier his task became. But even as he worked, even as the way opened slowly before him, Nathan felt no closer to the light. Something was wrong, somewhere. Some immovable barrier seemed to block his way and his awareness of this situation distressed him greatly and kept him from any lasting peace.

Once, it happened that he revisited a place and some people he had left under unhappy circumstances some years before. He found himself reacting to the situation as he would have before he met the man. He found himself filled with selfishness, with anger, resentment and pain. An old friend told him, "You see, Nathan, your present life may have changed but these things are very deep-seated. You must examine them, discover their causes and then, with all your heart, forgive anyone who may have offended you in the past." Nathan wept and told his companion, "These things are so deep-seated I do not understand them. They must be rooted near the very heart

of the mountain. How can I ever hope to chisel them out?"
In his misery, his thoughts turned to the man and some of
the words he remembered, "You must be true to your own
self, to the God within you, Who sees all and knows all.
How long will you carry this pain around inside you, thinking no one sees?" And some other words also came to him
at this time, "God resides in every heart. If you know this,
really know this in your heart of hearts, how can you hurt
the feelings of anyone?"

Sometime later that night, when Nathan returned in
very low spirits to his own home, he had a strange dream.
He dreamed he was a small child who stood with his father outside the shimmering gate of a vast, golden palace.
The child was weeping inconsolably. The father was loving, but firm. "But I don't want to go," pleaded the child
miserably, "I love it here and I see you quite often."
"There is no choice, my son," the father replied, "Even
this palace is not your true home. I want you to come all
the way back to stay with me forever and this is the only
way you can do that." "How long must I be gone?" sobbed
the child, "I'm afraid I won't be able to live away from
here and you." "I will grant you two boons, child. Illusion
will quickly wear thin for you down there and a striving
heart will hasten the journey." Abject, but obedient, he
clung to his father's hands and took one last look at the
radiant splendor he had called home for so long. "Go,"
He told him, gently releasing his hands, "The stars are
fixed, the family chosen, the pattern laid down. At the end

of the pattern you will begin your return. Do not tarry, my son, I will be waiting for you." And as the child looked, his father's face outshone all the glory around them. He took one last breath of that fragrant, ringing air, tore his eyes from his father's face, hurled himself into the dark well which lay at their feet and was born into the physical world.

Nathan awoke in a paroxysm of pain. Great cries of rage rent the air. *"I didn't want to be born, oh, God! I did not want to be born!"* Beside himself with all this never-released emotion, Nathan threw on some clothes and flung himself out of the house and into the woods which surrounded it. He ran through the bushes, not caring if his sleeves were torn or his boots became muddy. His head was in a frenzy; so much insight was coming to him at once. Frequently he stopped and screamed at the top of his lungs. The pain and anger seemed to come all the way up from his toes. He saw clearly for the very first time the buried feelings of hatred and resentment toward God and man that he had carried around in his heart and had tried to conceal from himself, from God and from others for so long. He felt sick. He recognized the feelings, he acknowledged how he had used them to withdraw from the world and his fellow men in a most unnatural way. And he realized with mounting horror that any such feelings were always against God, not man, and he trembled to see the depths of his willful separation.

With another great cry Nathan threw himself on the

ground and lay there, sobbing his heart out. He understood he must now joyfully embrace the whole creation,
for God's sake, just as he had willfully rejected it in the
past for his own. With his face against the earth, he begged
the man to intercede for him, to forgive him his folly and
grant him the gift of forgiveness for others. And soon his
whole being was bathed, yes, one might even say baptized
with the waters of total forgiveness and love.

And in the mountain of himself, the last great stone
was rolled away forever with a sound like thunder and
Nathan beheld the light of many suns once more. The walls
which had confined it seemed to vanish into nothingness
and all was light, all around him. With great relief and joy
Nathan entered into the light and embraced it and became
one with it thereafter.

HELPING EACH OTHER
TO FIND GOD

THERE WERE once two companions, a man and a woman, and they loved each other truly. At one time in their long life together, the woman received a summons, an imperious call to begin a long, long journey to a Place Far Away. The One Who called her was waiting for her there; He would send His two servants, Light and Music, to guide her on her way. The woman started off; she had no choice. She loved both music and light and she knew that she was going to love the One Who called for her more than all the world. The man, however, had received no call. Nor did he understand anything about the One Who called or about His two servants, Music and Light. But, because he loved the woman truly, he decided to accompany her on her journey.

Immediately, difficulties arose between them. The woman became so intoxicated by the prospect of the journey and by the two guides and became so involved in her own dreams of what awaited her in the Place Far Away that she sorely neglected her companion and eventually, because her mind was such, she began to consider him a positive impediment on the way. The man, in turn, became very angry. It seemed he was losing his beloved companion to something he understood nothing about. He began to say wounding things to her; he began to try to pull her back from making the journey. But she would look behind her and start in terror; to her eyes nothing was there—an empty space, an airy mist. For her the road opened only before her; there was no going back. They quarreled bitterly. The man threatened to leave. The woman pretended not to care but her heart was heavy within her all the same. She resolved to continue on, even if she were left alone.

Then the One Who had sent for her from the Place Far Away appeared before her in a vision. His beautiful face was very stern and by His manner she knew He was far from pleased, "What are you doing, traveling alone?" He asked the woman, "Have you no companion?"

"I had one," she whispered, awestruck at the sight of Him and terribly frightened at having so displeased Him, "But he went away."

"Go back to him, then," He told her abruptly. "The needs of your companion come first. Make him happy and then you may continue the journey. All you have to do is love him. And remember, the more you grow in love for each other, the more you will grow in love for me." And He was gone.

Filled with remorse for all her wrongheadedness and filled also with the desire to obey the One Who had sent for her at any cost, the woman hastened back to where the man sat, dreaming by a river. "I haven't been able to see you very well for a while," she said softly, "I'm so sorry I've hurt you; I've had such blinders on. I think they're gone, now." She went and kneeled at his feet and looked up into his face. "I still love you truly," she said. The man looked down at her, his brow still darkened with pain. "I don't believe you," he said, "You'll have to show me. Only time will prove the truth—or falsehood—of what you say."

And they began their life together once more. The woman knew that somehow she was still on the journey, but she went nowhere and the man became increasingly trustful and content. If the woman did occasionally lapse into her old dreams, the man snatched her out of them, sometimes angrily, sometimes sorrowfully. "We must always be completely open toward each other," he told her, "I need you to be here with me, not off in a dream." Often she cried in a curious combination of pain and thanksgiving; it seemed she was far from her journey to see the One Whom she had come to love more than all the world, and yet she understood that her companion was helping her to make the journey by forcing her to obey His wishes. And she wanted to obey; even when her foolish mind rebelled, her heart wanted to obey. The woman understood that she did not get away with anything. If she faltered at all, the man was there to chastise her, to demand changes, to push her forward again.

This process went on for some time. As the woman's attention became more and more focused on her companion and less and less focused on herself, the realization came to her that her companion was none other than the One Who had sent for her Himself, in another form, and she was overcome, overwhelmed with feelings of thankfulness for such a great gift; without her companion, she could not have begun the journey at all. And if she had, she would have made many wrong turns, often unwittingly, without him. Over and over again it was his criticism, his perception which kept her on the main road. All his prodding and pushing had been to open her up to the true beginning—passage through the first gate—to find the One standing there, arms outstretched, His face streaming rays of love and joy.

"I've brought her," says the man.

"You've done well, my son," replies the One. "Now, each of you take one of my hands; we will make the rest of the journey together."

DON'T GO AWAY

THERE WAS once a great king who had a beautiful daughter. He lavished presents on her, gave her everything she wanted, instructed her, cared for her, protected her, embraced her—in few words, he loved her very much. And the princess? she bloomed like a daisy in the summer sun. For years their lives went on in this manner, while the princess was growing up, until a day came when the king found himself musing as he strolled in his favorite rose garden, "I know my daughter loves me, but . . . I wonder how much she loves me." The question would not leave his mind and so he decided to find out the answer as quickly as possible. In the darkest hour of the night, he set out from the palace accompanied by a few trusted servants to pay a visit of undetermined length to his son in a country far away. He left instructions with his ministers that the princess was not to be told of his whereabouts until she had discovered for herself that he was no longer in the palace.

Now the princess was a very sensible person as well as a very sensitive one and when she went in to breakfast the following morning and found no customary greeting from her loving father, she passed the omission off as something of no consequence; her father was obviously busy with matters of state and would find time to see her later in the day. But after dancing lessons, geography lessons and lunch had passed without her catching so much as a glimpse of his face, she began to be stricken with pangs of conscience. "Perhaps I have displeased him, somehow," she concluded unhappily, "If that is so I must find him and apologize and try to make amends." With these thoughts, the princess went out to look for the king.

The first place she looked was in his favorite rose garden. The effect of his constant presence hung in the air; it was as strong as the scent of roses, but his royal form was nowhere to be seen. The princess sighed and began her search in earnest.

From the council chamber to the throne room, through seemingly endless corridors leading to dining halls, ball rooms, sculleries, pantries and kitchens, in the palace chapel—she looked everywhere; she asked everyone. And when at last she was satisfied that she had left no door unopened, no chair or bed unexamined, she sank down in tears on the palace steps and accepted the fact that her father was really and truly gone.

All day the ministers had watched the movements of the princess with sympathy and concern and when they perceived that she had fulfilled the king's condition, they went to her and told her that he had indeed gone away the previous night to visit her brother in his kingdom far away. The princess was very grateful for the information but she could not understand why such a journey would be kept a secret—there were no secrets between her father and herself, or so she had always thought. But eventually her sad face brightened as she thought of all the things she could do while he was away and, "Surely," she comforted herself, "He will not be gone for very long."

For a while, the princess remained quite busy and happy. She kept up with all her lessons, learned new dances, entertained guests and suitors as her father had taught her. She continued with all the responsibilities of her young life until she began to notice a change in her attitude toward all these things. At first, it was a very subtle change, too subtle to be remarked upon. Her interest in her surroundings diminished; her attention would not remain fixed on anything she undertook to do. Gradually everything became shadowy, ephemeral without her father's presence to brighten it, give it substance. Then she began to feel that she could not take her suitors seriously without her father's wise council to guide her. How completely she had depended on him! There seemed to be little purpose to life without him. Tears came easily to her eyes; she began to wander around the palace with a heavy heart.

She determined to write her father a letter. It said that everything was fine at home. It conveyed best wishes and much affection to her brother and hopes for a pleasant stay which she wished might soon be over. The letter was sent off; she eagerly awaited her father's answer. But none came.

Days dragged into weeks with no word and no sign. The grief-stricken condition of the princess worsened. Now everything she saw, everything she did, everything she heard only served to remind her of her absent father. She continued with her work, albeit less than half-heartedly, because she was a dutiful daughter, but there was no pleasure in it and the day soon came when her flowing tears soaked the yarns and canvas shrinking the one and warping the other so badly that even needlework, a favorite pastime, became impossible to do.

She wrote the king a second letter. Again she told him that all was well at home and sent affectionate greetings to her brother. But this time she admitted that she missed her father greatly and begged him to come home soon. This letter was dispatched. Surely these words would call forth a response! Again, none came; not a word, not a sign.

In the weeks that followed, the princess became inconsolable. Now she rarely left her tower room except to make a daily pilgrimage down into her father's rose garden where she would sit for a time, lost to the world. Most of the day and far into the night she sat by her window looking out to the east—the direction of her brother's kingdom and of her father's longed-for return.

She neglected her studies and lessons; she sent her suitors away. She refused to see visitors. Nothing could take her mind from thoughts of her father. Memories of their years together flooded both her waking hours and her dreams. At last, she began to neglect herself. Why should she look beautiful or act graceful or cultivate an intelligent mind or an artistic talent if there was no reason for doing so, no one to take pleasure in her? In fact, why should she eat? Why should she live?

The whole palace was concerned about her. The ministers stroked their beards and looked very grave; the maids shook their heads sorrowfully and dabbed at their eyes with the corners of their starched white aprons. Not a few commented with envy or scorn that her love knew no bounds.

In this desperate condition, the princess wrote a third letter to the king. It was very brief. It said, "If you care to see me alive, come home immediately. I cannot bear to live another day without you."

This letter was sent posthaste and the princess languished in bed for the rest of the day, too exhausted even to sit by the window at her customary vigil.

However, early the next morning the princess awoke with a feeling of great hope. In her heart she knew the king was coming at last. With unaccustomed strength and determination, she got out of bed and bathed and dressed in her most beautiful gown. She had decided to go forth to meet her father as he returned. "He will be hungry and thirsty after that long journey," she thought, and packed a small hamper with bread and fruit and a jug of spring water before she left the palace. Plucking one perfect red rose from his favorite garden and twining it in her dark hair, she set out onto the road.

From the palace gate the road stretched for miles across a flat, barren plain. The princess had to walk slowly for she was very weak. As she walked, she became aware of many loose stones lying around in the road. "These are not good for the horses' hooves," she remarked. "Suppose my father's horse stumbled and caused him to fall." It was a dreadful thought. Immediately she set down the hamper and began to clear the road of all the stones. In a short time under the hot sun the effort became too much for her; she grew increasingly faint and dizzy and finally crumpled into a little blue heap in the middle of the road.

In her unconscious state, even with her ears so close to the ground, she did not hear the thundering hooves making haste across that great plain. She did not feel strong arms lift her tenderly into the saddle to continue the journey home.

Gently her father lifted her down from his horse and carried her into the palace. Carefully he laid her down in a soft bed among silken cushions. And there he fed her a nourishing broth and some bits of bread with his own hands.

As soon as she was able to speak, the princess clasped

the king's hands to her heart and whispered, "Oh father, don't go away again, please, I beg you, don't ever go away."

Her father answered, his heart in his eyes, "Do not worry, beloved child of mine, this will never happen again."

And the princess? she bloomed like a daisy in the summer sun.

SET YOUR HOUSE IN ORDER

PARTWAY up the mountainside, the Pilgrim lay sprawled in the rubble. Trembling, miserable and unable to go any further, he was too exhausted even to move his face aside in the dirt. He lay there, trying with all his might to dispel the shadows before his eyes which had caused his fall. But the shadows would not go away. They clung to his eyes, to the space behind his eyes; they held him fast. At length, the Pilgrim groaned and cried aloud, "Lord, what is to become of me? I am beseiged; I cannot move!"

Suddenly there was a great stillness around him and a great warmth. Something touched his outstretched hand. The Pilgrim slowly roused himself and looked up, squinting through the ceaseless flow of shadows around his head. His Lord stood before him, a man like any other man, except for the great stillness, except for the great warmth

which surrounded him. On his face was a look of such
profound understanding and compassion, the Pilgrim wept
anew to see it.

"I wanted so much to come to You," he sobbed, "I
started out so boldly, with such zeal . . ."

"What of your house?" asked the Lord.

"Oh, that place! I left it long ago." The Pilgrim shud-
dered at the memory of it . . . "It was too dark and gloomy
and cold."

The look of compassion deepened on the Lord's face.
"Dear friend," He murmured, "Obviously it hasn't left
you. Matters are not at rest there or you would not be
beset by shadows now. You must set your house in order
before you can come to me."

"Oh, no," moaned the Pilgrim, "I don't want to go all
the way back down there. It's so far behind me now and
. . . and . . . there are rooms in it I have never entered
. . . Please help me to continue on my way up the mountain; don't send me back down there!"

"Beloved friend, there is no other way," replied the
Lord. "Your house must be in order, *completely* in order,
before you can come to me. Look, what a paltry self you
bring me! a weak and fearful creature who stumbles at
mere shadows. Is it not said, thou shalt love thy Lord with
all thy heart, with *all* thy soul, with *all* thy mind and with
all thy strength? Come to me in fulness, not in fear. Go
and open all those doors, one by one; fill the place with
light; sweep out every corner until there is no darkness

anywhere. When the task is done, I myself will come and get you."

The Pilgrim wept and stormed and begged and wrung his hands, to no avail. His Lord's words were hard, the very last words he had wanted to hear. But instead of sympathizing, the figure before him grew stern and commanded him: "I tell you, set your house in order or journey not toward Me." And with this final pronouncement, He was gone.

Teeth chattering and limbs shaking, but fire burning in his heart, the Pilgrim made his way slowly back down the mountainside. The air around him became increasingly dense with shadows until he found himself flailing his arms continuously to keep any open vision as he retraced his steps toward home.

Wearily he turned out the key from its hiding place in an old flowerpot, unlocked the front door, went in and sat down. Fresh tears fell as he looked around him at the dust, the cobwebs, the cold hearth. But, "Lo! I am with you always!" sang to him suddenly out of the fire in his heart and the Pilgrim knew, even though at the moment he hated being here, that he had come to the right place and that, somehow, everything would be all right.

It took months for the Pilgrim to do even the most superficial cleaning. He had always thought he kept a decent house but closer examination revealed many unexpected messes he had never noticed before.

And it took nearly a year before the Pilgrim had gained

enough courage to stand in front of the first of the four unopened doors, knowing now that he was strong enough to open it and enter the room there and face and conquer, nay, even befriend whatever awaited him there.

Shadows crowded around him, in front of his eyes, in the space behind his eyes and suddenly he was seized with terror, shaking and choking with it and from the depths of his heart came the cry, "I'm scared! I'm so scared!" And with the strength of this cry he opened the door and rushed inside. Instantly all the shadows vanished and he saw to his amazement a shadowy figure, very like himself, cowering and quaking and sniveling in the middle of a dismal, empty room. The Pilgrim's heart went out to the poor creature. "Come," he said, "You shall sup with me tonight." And he took it by the hand and led it back along the corridor into the central chamber in the house where there was a long table set in front of a blazing fire.

And then he went back to the first room and opened all the windows and lit all the lamps and washed and scrubbed and scoured until there wasn't the shadow of a shadow of the fear that had lived in there so long.

The Pilgrim lived with fear for some time and they became intimate friends, until there was nothing the Pilgrim did not know about fear. But, strangely enough, the longer their friendship continued, the fainter the shadowy figure became until one day, in the bright sunlight which came through the huge skylight in the central chamber, fear was not there at all. And the Pilgrim set his jaw and turned his attention and his footsteps toward the second door.

He stood in front of this one, knowing that he now had the strength to open it and enter the room and face and conquer, aye, even befriend whatever awaited him there. But again shadows crowded around him, in front of his eyes, in the space behind his eyes and suddenly he was filled with pain, until every muscle, every nerve, every organ in his body was shrieking, "I hurt! Oh, I hurt!" and with the strength of this cry, he opened the door and rushed inside. Immediately all the shadows vanished and he found to his surprise a shadowy figure, very like himself, doubled up and writhing on the bare floor. It was clutching its stomach as though it had a spear or an arrow in it which it was struggling to remove. "Oh, you poor thing!" gasped the Pilgrim, "Come along out of here and let me try to help you." He put his arms gently around the creature and led it into the light and warmth of the great central chamber in which he spent most of his time.

Then the Pilgrim went back to the second room and opened all the windows and lit all the lamps and dusted and swept and polished until there wasn't the shadow of a shadow of the pain that had lived in there so long.

Pain and the Pilgrim spent much time together. They, too, became intimate friends until there was no sorrow, no anguish in this world the Pilgrim did not know. But, strangely enough, the longer their friendship continued, the fainter the shadowy figure became until one day, as evening light shone through the sparkling windows on the western side of the fireplace, pain was not there at all. And the Pilgrim took a deep breath and made his way toward the third door.

This time the shadows assailed him in the corridor and raged around his head until he almost lost his courage, thought he was going mad and turned to flee into the safe familiarity of the central chamber. But, "Stop!" sang the voice in the depths of his burning heart, "Have you forgotten I am with you always? And, Beloved, who do you think is *really* doing all this work?" Both ashamed and heartened, the Pilgrim reset his steps grimly toward the third door. The heat was overpowering and it was nothing like the warmth of his Lord. It was a red-hot blast, a passionate fury which engulfed him as he stood there. From his fingertips, his toes, his bowels, his entire being he felt the violence boiling up and he opened his throat and roared, "I'm angry, I'm so ANGRY!" and he threw the door open and strode inside. The heat stopped abruptly. The shadowy leonine figure which looked just like him snarling and pacing the floor in the dimly lighted room did not surprise the Pilgrim. "Come on," he said bravely, taking a firm grip on the creature's arm, "You and I will have much to talk about."

Well, it took a longer time than either fear or pain did, but the Pilgrim eventually made friends with anger, too. And at last the shadowy figure that was the Pilgrim's anger disappeared from his house in much the same way as fear and pain.

This left only one more unopened door, but it was many years before the Pilgrim could bring himself to face it. One day he was thinking of his Lord and remembering that He had said the house must be completely in order before . . . before anything really good could happen and, as the fire in his heart burned particularly brightly that day, he found himself stiffening his shoulders for this last, most difficult foray.

The shadows were more than shadows which clung to his eyes, to the space behind his eyes this time; they were shapes, moving, sinuous, twining shapes, like temple reliefs, like old frescoes and paintings, like words from books given bodies and he felt his skin prickle and go hot and the rest of his body throbbed with delicious, delightful sensations. "Oh," he groaned, "I want it, I need it, I love it!" and he threw himself into the room.

The heavy scent of musk and sandalwood hung in the air. Candles burned. By their flickering light the Pilgrim could make out a strange, naked form, half male and half female, which lay on an enormous bed in the center of the room. It was tossing and writhing from side to side as though both it and the soft surface under it were on fire. It looked longingly at the Pilgrim and held out its arms to him.

Slowly the Pilgrim advanced until he stood beside the bed staring down at its restless occupant. Then slowly, but very firmly, he shook his head. "I'm glad I can finally face you," he began, "and I'm glad the time has come when even you and I can become friends. But I will not stay here; you, too, must come with me." So saying, he gathered the feverish creature up in his arms and walked out of that stifling room and down the hall toward the coolness and the clear light of the great central chamber.

No one knows how long the Pilgrim's friendship with physical desire lasted but let it be known that he learned all that he needed to learn. And when the amorous being that was the Pilgrim's own sensuality finally disappeared into the bright air as the others had done before it and the house had no darkness in it, anywhere, at all, the Pilgrim was at peace and thought his task was done.

It was not so. The Pilgrim lay in front of the hearth one night and in a dream he saw a small door opening and a long, bony hand reaching around to grasp his hand. In this dream the Pilgrim tried to close that door and there had been no lock on it and the bony hand had reached for him again.

The Pilgrim awakened in a cold sweat with his heart pounding. "It was Death," he said to himself. "Fool that I am, I have not yet made a friend of Death!" And without a moment's hesitation, he scrambled up into an old forgotten attic on one end of the house and opened the fifth and very last door . . .

But instead of bony fingers and the dampness of the tomb, there was a familiar stillness and a singing light. "It is I, Beloved," said the Lord, "I promised I would come for you when your house was completely in order and so I have."

His face radiant with the fulness of his understanding and his heart filled with love and trust, the Pilgrim went back up the mountainside in the company of his Lord.

BEFORE THE WEDDING

IT WAS THE FEAST of their betrothal and everyone was happy. The husband-to-be sat like a king on a throne and all the guests thronged around him, admiring. The bride-to-be was young and very shy: she stole many a glance at this man she was to marry, thinking all the while, "How is it that I of all people am fortunate enough to marry this great one; see how beautiful he is and how kind! How lucky I am!" And the husband-to-be, as though he could read her thoughts, returned all those glances, feeding fire with far greater fire . . .

Once, during the festivities, he called her to his side and heaped gifts upon her. One gift was three gowns which fit over one another.* The outer one was a magnificent, long robe made of heavy red brocade. It was embroidered richly with gold and silver threads and with pearls and precious stones. The second was a simpler gown of soft, grey satin. It, too, was long and rich-looking, but it had no ornaments on it. The third, the innermost garment, was a plain, short silk shift of dazzling whiteness. When she was dressed in these and came hesitantly before him again, he filled her arms with ripe fruit** and laughed into her eyes. "I think you have everything you need now," he said merrily. Then the little bride-to-be became intoxicated, overflowing with love and joy, and the fire in her grew and grew. "All I want in the world is to be with him, forever." And she danced her joy before him.

It was such a happy time.

Then the bride-to-be thought to herself, "But he has said nothing yet about our marriage plans; when will that be?" And she plucked at his sleeve and murmured, ". . . and our marriage?" "Soon, soon," he replied easily, "I'll be around." And with this vague reply the bride-to-be had to be satisfied.

He *was* around; she saw him from time to time and each time she was with him his glances kindled her more. But the times of separation grew increasingly painful for the

* A Christian source, St. John of the Cross, has mentioned three similar robes as symbols for the divine attributes of faith, hope and love. The red gown represents love.

** The ripe fruit symbolizes the fulfillment of all earthly desires.

bride-to-be and she longed for some definite word of their marriage.

Once when they were together and she was weeping over the length of their most recent separation, he took her on his lap and comforted her like a small child. He told her, "There is a way to be with me all the time if you really want to be. There is a secret stairway leading to my home. When you really want to be with me forever, climb that stair. It is one hundred steps high and very, very narrow and you must leave everything behind and climb all the way to the top without thinking once of anything but me." He stroked her hair and smiled down at her, his face radiant with love. "I'll be waiting for you there," he said, "Rest assured of that."

She heard his words, but she didn't pay close attention: it was enough that she was with him again for that time and that the fire in her steadily grew and grew.

He was around, I say; they saw each other more or less frequently and then one day, without any warning at all, the bride-to-be received word that her beloved had suddenly gone home.

She was bereft; she was inconsolable. She could not sleep or eat; she wept continuously. It seemed to her that all the light, all the reason for living had gone out of the world. Could it be that he did not want to marry her, after all, she wondered. No, no; the memory of his countless radiant glances and of all his loving care assured her that could not be true. Well then, could it be that he didn't think she cared enough to want to marry him? That thought was even more painful to her than the first . . .

For a time she wandered around in this sad world with a broken heart, wondering where "home" was to her beloved and how she could possibly follow him there. And then one day, in all her misery and loneliness, she finally remembered what he had told her that time when he had held her and comforted her like a small child. He had told her the same thing at other times, too, she realized, but she had been forgetful, so forgetful! There was a stairway, one hundred steps high, very narrow . . . if she wanted to see him she had to climb the entire stair and think of nothing but him . . . All the time he had been around she could have been with him in this way but it had not seemed so important, then. Now, now that there was no other way to see him . . .

She sat down, very quietly, and suddenly, through her tears, she saw the stair. And it *was* very narrow and it *was* very steep: she could not see the top of it, but the memory of her beloved's glances seized and held her and the fire inside her burned and burned. She thought to herself for the millionth time, "All I want is to be with him; all I want in the world is to be with him, forever." And she began to climb.

It was not easy. In fact, it was the most difficult thing she had ever attempted. She soon found that, for all her love, other matters kept crowding into her mind causing her to slip and slide back down the stairs over and over again. But her love was strong and ever-growing and she would not be discouraged. After all, had he not assured her repeatedly that he was waiting for her at the top of the stair? Gradually she began to forget all that was going on in the world around her as she bent more and more concentrated attention toward learning to climb that stair. And little by little, love crowded out all other thoughts in her mind until she was left at last with only memories of her beloved's radiant face in her mind and a burning desire to see him again in her heart.

And the day finally came when she did attempt the stairway and managed to climb all the way to the top without thinking of anything at all—even once—but her beloved.

Lo and behold, at the one hundredth step a door opened and light streamed out. There he stood like a king at a palace gate, his arms opened wide. "I knew you would come one day," he said, laughing into her eyes as he drew her toward himself inside the door. Then he turned and signaled for the marriage ceremony to begin.